THE
LIFE

OF

JACK RANN,

OTHERWISE

Sixteen-String Jack,

THE

NOTED HIGHWAYMAN;

WHO WAS EXECUTED AT TYBURN,

NOVEMBER 30, 1774.

London:

PRINTED BY AND FOR HODGSON AND CO.

No. 10, NEWGATE STREET.

Sixpence.

THE

LIFE

OF

JACK RANN.

———

THIS unfortunate object was born of very industrious honest parents, at a village near Bath; but
being in indigent circumstances, and having a large
family, they could afford to give them but a very
scanty portion of learning: but whatever their inabi-
lities in circumstances prevented their inclination
from accomplishing in that respect, their industrious
example might have been a pattern for every one
of their children to have followed; and if the hero
of the succeeding narrative had been blessed with
grace sufficient to have followed so virtuous a
pattern, he might have been one of the most happy
of men, and have prevented that punishment which
has so justly fallen upon himself, and brought disgrace upon his nearest friends, who felt more for his
sufferings than he did for himself.

He was not, as some of his late predecessors in infamy were, inured to vice from his infancy, but brought up to industry: for some time, he obtained a livelihood by vending goods, which he drove round the city and adjacent country on an ass, and by so doing, attracted the attention of a lady of distinction who happened to be at Bath, who took Jack Rann into her service when he was about twelve years of age; and his behaviour was such, that he became the favourite of his mistress and of his fellow servants.

At length he came to London, and got employment as a helper in the stables, at Mr. Brook's, in Brook's Mews, at the west end of the town, in which station he bore a good character. He then became the driver of a post chaise; after which he was servant to an officer in the army, and in both these stations he was well spoken of. About four years before his execution, he was coachman to a gentleman of fortune near Portman-square, and it was after this period that he dressed in a manner which gave rise to the appellation of Sixteen-string Jack, by wearing eight strings at each knee.

After living in the service of several noblemen, he lost his character, and turned pick-pocket, in company with three fellows named Jones, Claton, and College.

Sixteen-string Jack was about twenty-four years of age, about five feet five inches high, wore his own hair, of a light brown colour, which combed over his forehead; remarkably clean, and particularly neat in his dress; and besides the strings at his knees, he wore a peculiar hat, with strings and a button on the crown: he was straight, of a genteel carriage, and made a very handsome appearance.

However, the time of his commencing villain, is supposed to be about two years before his exit, soon after which he was found in Tothill-Fields Bridewell, charged on suspicion of robbing a post-chaise on Hounslow Heath; but the parties not being able to prove the identity of his person, and nothing farther appearing against him, he was discharged from confinement.

During his being in custody in Bridewell, he contracted an acquaintance with some of his own profession, who all having the good fortune to be dismissed for want of sufficient evidence to convict them, were again set at large, to levy contributions on the public.

With some of those he entered into solemn engagements to be true and stedfast to each other: nor was the fulfilling of these covenants ever wanting on his part; for, at the various times he had been in danger and distress, and strongly solicited to make an impeachment of his accomplices, by which he might have made considerable advantages, he always nobly refused, saying,—" That he always kept company with gentlemen, on whose honour and fidelity he had the strongest reliance ; he would never be the first who should bring disgrace upon so sacred a name, by renouncing those engagements which every man of honour ought to keep inviolate."   Numerous were the robberies committed by Sixteen-string Jack and his associates, soon after their release.

In December sessions, 1773, John Rann, William Davis, otherwise Scarlet, David Munro, and John Saunders, were indicted for robbing Mr. Simmonds, passenger in the Hampstead stage-coach, of one guinea and three shillings and six-pence.

Mr. Simmonds deposed, that coming to town from Hampstead on the thirteenth of November, a little before six in the evening, the coach was stopped by five people, who took from him the money mentioned in the indictment, noticing the particular circumstance that they behaved very civil, and rather seemed to beg for money than use any violent means, though he observed a pistol in one of their hands ; but being rather dark, he would not swear positively to their persons.

Thomas Shed, the coachman, deposed, that the

coach was stopped by five people, three met him on the road, and two came out of a field; one of them held a pistol up to him, and said, " If you do not stop, I will blow your brains out:" upon which he desired him to put the pistol down, which he accordingly did, and behaved exceeding civil.

Mr. Davis deposed, that he was in the coach with Mr. Clark and Mr. Simmonds when the coach was stopped; that Mr. Clark bid the coachman go on, but one of them said, if he did, he would blow his brains out, and that he was robbed of three shillings; that Munro held his hat for the money, and he was leaning out of the window when he gave it him, but could not particularly distinguish the colour of his clothes.

John Clarke, in consequence of an information made at Sir John Fielding's office of this robbery, went on the road that night, but not finding any suspected persons, they returned to town, and searched several disorderly houses: at a house in Knave's Acre they found the four prisoners, together with one Scott, who was afterwards admitted an evidence for the crown.

Richard Bond deposed, that he was with Clarke when they found the prisoners, soon after the robbery; and, on searching them, they found some shot in the pocket of Munro, and a pistol in the room, loaded with a slug, upon which they were taken into custody, and committed for further examination, except Scott, who was dismissed the next morning.

However, Scott surrendered himself again on the Wednesday following, and desired to be admitted an evidence, which was accordingly granted, and on the trial deposed, that the prisoners and he made an agreement to go out on the above Saturday, when they met a coach a little on this side the lane leading to Chalk Farm; that they robbed the passengers of one pound six shillings and sixpence; that Saunders held the pistol to the coachman, and Munro received the money in his hand; then going a little further, they met a horse, and a man standing by it, whose money they likewise demanded: they then returned to town, and went to the house in Knave's Acre about ten o'clock the same evening; went into the little room by themselves, and were there when Bond and Clarke came in, who searched them, and told them they were out upon an information.

In their defence they pleaded their ignorance; but no creditable evidence being given sufficient to validate the account of the accomplice, and several persons appearing to their character, they were all acquitted.

In April sessions, 1774, John Ran, William Clayton, and Robert Shepherd, were twice indicted for two separate highway robberies, but had the good fortune to get clear of them both; but a detainer being lodged, and an indictment found against Shepherd, for a robbery in the Duke of Manchester's stables of some wearing apparel, and other things, he was convicted to be transported, by which means Jack was deprived of one of his principal accomplices.

After his acquittal, he was always received with open arms by some one or other of those ladies, who were his constant companions; but their support being very temporary, and he being given to much extravagance and pleasure, was soon under the necessity of following his usual profession.

And on Saturday the twenty-first of May, Rann and one of his companions being on a party of business, stopped John Devall, Esq. who was in a single horse chaise, near the Nine-Mile Stone on the Hounslow Road, and robbed him of his watch and seven guineas. He was at this time engaged in an amorous intercourse with Miss Smith, at whose lodgings he came about an hour after the above robbery, and gave her the watch and five guineas. The watch was offered to Mr. Allam, by Eleanor Roche, who being questioned as to the manner of her becoming possessed of it, acknowledged that she was commissioned to dispose of it by Miss Smith. A warrant was obtained, by virtue of which these ladies were apprehended, and taken before Sampson Wright, Esq. when informations in writing were taken from them respectively.

On the Monday se'nnight Rann was apprehended, and on the following Wednesday put to the bar in Bow-street; the watch was produced and sworn to, both by the maker and Mr. Devall, the owner, who, however, would not positively swear to the identity of Rann, but said, that from his appearance and manner, he believed him to be one of the men who robbed him.

Miss Smith was now called, and though she had, upon her examination before Justice Wright, positively sworn that she received the watch from Rann, she now disavowed every syllable contained in her information upon oath, and pleaded very hard to be excused saying any thing against the prisoner, to whom she declared herself to be an entire stranger. There appeared to be a mixture of real concern in the behaviour of Miss Smith; for being asked if she knew Rann, in a scarcely audible voice, answered in the negative, and could not for a long time be prevailed upon to cast her eyes towards the bar; at length, after being indulged with a tumbler of water, and allowed a few minutes to collect her spirits, she very attentively cast her eyes upon our hero, and

then firmly persisted in the declaration of not having
the least knowledge of his person; at the same time
alledging, that the abrupt manner of the peace
officers coming into her apartment, threw her into
such extreme confusion, that without thought or
design, she acknowledged receiving the watch from
Rann, whose name she merely pitched upon by
accident. She said, that when she persisted in her
charge against him on her examination before Justice
Wright, she was divested of reason; and begged to
revoke the whole of her deposition, which she declared
to be false in every instance. This tale was neither
suggested, nor executed with sufficient art to elude
the penetration of the magistrates, who ordered
Miss Smith behind the bar, to answer the charge of
receiving the watch from John Rann, knowing the
same to be stolen.

Roche was now sworn, and she deposed, that on
the day of Mr. Devall's robbery, Smith informed her
that she expected Jack to bring her some money in
the evening, and that he accordingly came about ten
o'clock, and retired with Smith for nearly half an
hour; that soon after his departure, she confessed
having received a watch and five guineas from
him, saying that he had that evening taken them
from a gentleman on the highway; and that she
carried the watch to Mr. Allam, by the express desire
of Miss Smith.

Being asked by Sir John Fielding, if he had any thing to offer in extenuation of the charge alleged against him, Rann replied, " I know no more of the matter than your worship." Mr. Devall and Mr. Allam were bound over to prosecute Rann as the principal, and Miss Smith as an accomplice, after the fact, and Roche was bound to give evidence against them.

At his coming into the office, he behaved rather with indecency, and his appearance was such as drew the eyes of all present towards him. His answers to the questions asked him, seemed to convince the auditors, that he possessed a matchless share of effrontery, rather than to invalidate the charge adduced against him ; and, in short, his behaviour during his whole examination, was, in every instance, deserving reprehension.

At the ensuing sessions of the Old Bailey, Rann was indicted for the robbery of Mr. Devall, and Miss Smith was indicted for receiving the watch of Rann, knowing it to be stolen.

Mr. Devall deposed, that about nine o'clock on the 21st of May, he was stopped by two men on horseback, near the Nine-Mile Stone, on this side Hounslow; that he was in a one-horse chaise; that he gave one of the robbers seven guineas, and the other his watch ; but being dark he could not distinguish their persons, or even their clothes; that he advertised his watch, with a reward of four guineas, if it was brought to Mr. Allam, the maker.

Mr. Allam, junior, deposed, that the watch was brought to his father's house by Eleanor Roche.

Eleanor Roche deposed, that being at the house of the prisoner, Smith, she told her Jack was gone upon the road to get her some money, that she expected him home at ten o'clock; that he did come home within five minutes after, in a coach; and he gave Smith five guineas and the watch; that on the Sunday night following, when she was there, Smith had the watch by her side; that on Sir John Fielding's people searching the lodgings, Smith put the watch into this deponent's hand; that she, Roche, put the watch on a chair, and put the cover of the chair over it, so that it was not to be seen; that she afterwards talked with the prisoner, saying she did wrong to give her the watch, for she might have been brought into danger; to which Smith answered, " Oh, as you do not live with him, if I had given you fifty watches, you could come to no harm:" that when Rann came home he was in boots and spurs; and that this deponent went afterwards to Mr. Allam's, and gave information where the watch might be come at.

Rann, in his defence, said he knew nothing of the

robbery; that he had known Roche a considerable time, and that she had sworn against him through malice, because he would not take her into keeping; but that he had been a friend to her in many respects.

Roche acknowledged receiving some favours from a person at Epsom, but could not tell whether the prisoner was the person or not.

Catherine Smith, in her defence, said that she did not receive the watch from Rann, but from a person whom she met in the Strand, who took her to a tavern, and not having any money, took her directions to call for the watch, but did not come; and that Eleanor Roche extorted it from her maid, with whom she had left it in case the gentleman called for it. Nothing more appearing against them to support the charge, they were both acquitted.

Two or three days after his acquittal he engaged to sup with Miss ———, at her lodgings in Bow-street; but not being punctual to his appointment, the lady went to bed, and about midnight her lover arrived, but not being able to gain admittance at the door, he attempted to get in at the one pair of stairs window, and very nearly accomplished his purpose, when he was perceived by the watchman, who immediately took him into custody, and detained him till Wednesday following, when Miss ——— appeared in his behalf, and assured the bench that he could have had no felonious intention, as he only attempted to get into her apartment, where he knew himself to be a welcome guest, and would have gained a ready admission, had she not unfortunately fell asleep. No other charge being brought against him, he was dismissed, after having been exhorted in a very pathetic manner by Sir John Fielding to decline the vicious courses he had so long pursued, and apply himself to some honest, and less dangerous and disgraceful means of obtaining a livelihood.

The Sunday after this enterprise, our hero made his appearance at Bagnigge Wells, elegantly dressed in a scarlet coat, tambour waistcoat, white silk stockings, laced hat, &c. and some of the company knowing him, publicly challenged him, which he had the audacity not to deny. Having drank pretty freely, he became quarrelsome, and several scuffles ensued, in one of which he lost a ring from his finger, and when he discovered his loss, he said it was one evening's work, which he valued at a hundred guineas. He became at length so extremely troublesome, that part of the company agreed to turn him out of the house; but they met with so obstinate a resistance, that they were obliged to give up their design; when a number of young fellows attacked this magnanimous hero, and actually forced him through the window into the road. His mind seemed to be hurt more than his body by this rough treatment; for he exclaimed bitterly against the frequenters of Bagnigge Wells, for the indignity they had shewn to a gentleman of his character.

Some time after Rann had been tried for the robbery of Mr. Devall on the highway, he was arrested for thirty-three pounds, and not being able to pay the debt, or give bail for the action, he was committed to the Marshalsea prison. While he was in this situation, he was visited by a great number of girls of the town. His debt was soon paid, and he was released.

A short time after, Rann and two of his companions were at a public-house near Tottenham Court Road turnpike, when two sheriff's officers, who had a writ against Rann, entered the room and arrested him. As he had not money to pay the debt, he deposited his watch, and his two companions advanced three guineas, which, together, made more than the amount of the debt, and a balance, when the watch was redeemed, was to be returned to Rann; he said if the bailiffs would lend him five shillings, he would treat them with a crown's worth of punch. This being complied with, the liquor was called for, during the drinking which, Rann told the officers that they did not treat him like a gentleman. "When Sir John Fielding's people come after me," said he, "they use me genteelly; they only hold up a finger—beckon me—and I follow them as quietly as a lamb."

The officers being gone, Rann and his companions mounted their horses and rode off; but our hero returned in an hour or two, stopped at the turnpike, and asked the tollman if he had been wanted. "No," said the man.—"What, do not you know me?—Why," he said, "I am Sixteen-string Jack, the famous highwayman—Have any of Sir John Fielding's people been this way?"—"Oh! yes," cried the tollman, they have; some of them are but just gone through."—Rann replied, "If you see them again, tell them I am gone towards London," and rode off at his leisure.

But we shall now continue the narrative that leads to this unhappy object's conviction, of a charge brought against him for robbing the Reverend Doctor Bell on the highway, near Gunnersbury Lane.

Doctor Bell, in a circumstantial narrative, acquainted the Bench of Justices, at the public office in Bow-street, that between three and four o'clock in the afternoon, on Monday the twenty-sixth of September, as he was riding near Ealing, he observed two men rather of mean appearance, who rode past him; and that he remarked to himself, that they had suspicious looks; yet neither at that time, nor for some little time afterward, had he any idea of being robbed. At about half an hour after three, one of them, whom he believed (but could not swear) to be Rann, crossed the head of his horse, and de-

manded his money, saying, " Give it me, and tak
no notice, or I'll blow your brains out." The Doc
tor then offered him eighteen-pence, which was al
the silver he had : but in searching for more, th
highwayman found and took his watch.

On the evening of the day this robbery was com
mitted, between eight and nine o'clock, Eleano
Roche, (who was kept by Rann), and her maid
brought a watch to pledge with Mr. John Cordy,
pawnbroker, in Oxford Road, who suspecting i
was not honestly acquired, stopt it, and applied t
the maker, Mr. Grignion, of Russell-street, Cover
Garden, who informed him that it belonged t
Dr. Bell.

Mr. Clarke, a peace officer, deposed, that on goin
to Miss Roche's lodgings on the Monday nigh
in consequence of the hints obtained by Mr. Cordy
stopping the watch, he found there two pair o
boots, very wet and dirty, which had evidently bee
worn that day. Another peace officer waited a
Roche's lodgings till Rann and Collier came thithe
in consequence of which they were both appre
hended.

It likewise appeared in evidence on his examina
tion, that on the following morning (Tuesday,) tw
horses were brought to Miss Roche's lodgings, o
which the prisoners were again to have taken a rid

but the prisoners were then in custody. There could be no doubt but the horses were intended for the use of Rann and Collier, for it was proved that the latter paid for the hire of them; though both the prisoners denied knowing any thing about them.

Dr. Bell was clear in opinion, that Rann bore a strong resemblance to the man who robbed him, though he would not swear positively to his identity. On the strength of the above recited evidence, the prisoners were committed to Tothill Fields Bridewell; and Eleanor Roche was sent to Clerkenwell Bridewell, as the supposed receiver of Dr. Bell's stolen watch.

On Wednesday, October the 5th, John Rann, William Collier, and Eleanor Roche (together with Christian Stewart, Roche's servant girl,) were again brought to Bow-street, when Dr. Bell deposed, in substance, as he had done the preceding week, and positively swore that the stolen watch was his property.

Hannah Craggs swore to the being present at Miss Roche's lodgings, when the prisoners went away together on horseback, on the day of the robbery.

Mr. Cordy again proved the stopping of the Doctor's watch, when it was offered to him in pledge the same evening, by Miss Roche; but the most corroborating circumstance was given by William Hills, (servant to the Princess Amelia,) who swore to his having seen John Rann (whom he had long known) with a companion, ascending the hill at Acton, about twenty minutes before Dr. Bell was robbed; and this answered extremely well to the distance from Acton to the place where the robbery was committed.

At the examination, Christian Stewart behaved with great duplicity, pretending at first that she did not know either of the prisoners, though she afterwards acknowledged that she knew Collier; and from hence arose a very just suspicion that she was well acquainted with the parties, and the nature of their occupation.

As the present strength of evidence was thought sufficient, John Rann and William Collier were committed to Newgate to take their trials for highway robbery; Eleanor Roche to Clerkenwell Bridewell, and Christian Stewart to that of Tothill Fields, to be tried as accessaries after the fact.

In October sessions, John Rann and William Collier were indicted at the Old Bailey, for the above robbery of Dr. Bell, together with Eleanor Roche, as an accomplice after the fact, by receiving the watch from Rann, knowing it to have been stolen

Dr. Bell, in his evidence, proved the watch to be his property, and by a chain of concurrent circumstances, brought the charge home to the prisoners, except the particular point of swearing positively to their persons. But the court clearly viewing the fact in a proper light, gave a very elaborate and pathetic charge to the jury, which at once distinguished their knowledge of the laws, and their love of mercy, clearly drawing a line between circumstantial evidence and positive proof.

When the judge had given his charge to the jury, they withdrew for some time; but no proof being brought to invalidate the evidence given on the trial, they brought in the prisoners guilty, John Rann and William Collier to suffer DEATH, and Eleanor Roche to be transported for being an accessary after the robbery was committed, by receiving the watch.

Some circumstances appearing in Collier's favour during the course of the trial, he was, by compassion of the jury, recommended to the court for mercy; and there is more than probable reason to think Rann would have escaped the punishment of his crime this time, had not his character been so notoriously bad, and his name standing so often upon record at the Old Bailey.

When they were brought into court in order for trial, Rann behaved with a very careless and indifferent air, seeming entirely regardless of his truly critical and dangerous situation, and which all present could not behold without the deepest concern; his dress was entirely new: green coat, buckskin breeches, ruffled shirt, and hat bound round with silver strings.

Rann was so confident of being acquitted on his last trial, that he ordered a genteel supper to be provided for the entertainment of a number of his particular friends and associates on the joyful occasion. Alas! what was the disappointment of the company, when they heard the fate of the unhappy wretch. Riot was turned into mourning, and the madness of guilty joy, to the sullen melancholy of equally guilty grief.

On Tuesday, the 26th of October, 1774, John Rann, William Collier, and Eleanor Roche, received sentence at the Old Bailey, the two first to be executed at Tyburn, and the last to be transported for fourteen years. When Rann had received his sentence, he seemed by no means to be affected with it, but rather seemed to have a smile on his countenance, while his other companions appeared deeply affected with their crimes as well as punishment.

During his confinement, he lived a very gay and expensive life, being frequented by great numbers of his acquaintances of both sexes, to whom he always behaved in that same jocose manner as he was wont to do when more at large, having a number of entertainments, and servants to wait upon him.

At length, by the means of good advice, and the example of some who went out to suffer before him, he seemed entirely struck with a proper sense of his unhappy situation, and behaved to the last with becoming decency.

Rann's general character was that of a bold, ignorant fellow : he was fond of boasting of his exploits in all companies, without regard to his personal safety ; he was extremely apt to be quarrelsome when he was in liquor, and very fond of fighting with any man he might meet in the street. Miss Roche was a girl who having been early seduced from the paths of virtue, had lived with different men in various ranks of life, till she at length came to the knowledge of Rann. From the fate of this unhappy youth let others be taught never to embark in an illicit connexion with any woman of ill fame ; it is the ready and certain path to destruction, from which nothing can so effectually guard young men as a steady adherence to the rules of virtue and religion.

Rann's attachment to women of ill fame is by no means extraordinary for a man in his situation. The debauched mind has no idea of the purity of real love, and it is to be lamented that we have so few books in the English language calculated to inspire and direct this laudable passion. There is, however, one little pamphlet called the Lovers' New Guide, which exceeds every thing of the kind that has been written in the English or any other language; it contains very interesting letters on the subjects of love, courtship, and marriage; with dialogues, cards of compliments, and poems on the same important subject, and in fact a variety of that kind of writing which is calculated to teach the passions to move at the command of virtue. Young persons cannot purchase, or parents present a more admirable production, as a guide on the most important concerns of human life.

THE END.

Printed by Hodgson and Co. 10, Newgate Street.